W9-AVK-188
Public Library

# Parents in the Pigpen, Pigs in the Tub

*by* AMY EHRLICH

*pictures by* STEVEN KELLOGG

Dial Books for Young Readers *New York*

Published by Dial Books for Young Readers
A Division of Penguin Books USA Inc.
375 Hudson Street, New York, New York 10014


Designed by Jane Byers Bierhorst
Printed in the U.S.A.
First Edition
1 3 5 7 9 10 8 6 4 2

Library of Congress Cataloging in Publication Data
Ehrlich, Amy
Parents in the pigpen, pigs in the tub
Amy Ehrlich ; pictures by Steven Kellogg.
p. cm.
Summary : Tired of their usual routine, the farm animals insist on moving into the house, so the family decides to move into the barn. But eventually everyone tires of this new arrangement.
ISBN 0-8037-0933-1. ISBN 0-8037-0928-5 (lib. bdg.)
[1. Domestic animals—Fiction. 2. Farm life—Fiction. 3. Humorous stories.] I. Kellogg, Steven, ill. II. Title.
PZ7.E328Par 1993 [E]—dc20 91-15601 CIP AC

*The full-color artwork was prepared using ink and pencil line and watercolor washes. It was then color-separated and reproduced as red, blue, yellow, and black halftones.*

For Sophie and Amelia, who love our farm A.E.

To Arlen and Tatia, with love S.K.

It all began last summer when my little sister Millie left the pasture gate open. The animals got out and they saw us in the house.

"That sure looks better than the stuff they feed us," I heard one of the chickens say.

"Right," grumbled Bossy the cow.

"They got no flies in there neither," Baa-baa the black sheep said. "The flies in the barn this year are enough to drive me nuts."

We rounded up all the animals, and the next morning Pa got up at four, same as usual. He milked Bossy and sheared the sheep and slopped the pigs and fixed the fences and harnessed the workhorses and planted corn.

Back at the house he heard a knock at the door.
"I'm tired of living in a barn," said Bossy. "I want to move in here with you."

"Hold on just a minute. I'll talk to my wife," Pa said.

Ma had been up since four too. She'd fed the chickens and taken the ducks to the pond and weeded the garden and mopped the floor and fixed breakfast and done the laundry.

"Mary, come quick!" said Pa. "Bossy the cow wants to move in with us."

"Ids a white wif me."

"What was that?" asked Pa.

Ma took the clothespins out of her mouth. "I said it's all right with me. We're so busy, what's one more mouth to feed at the house?"

The next morning when Ma finished chores, the chickens followed her out of the chicken coop.

The chickens sat down with me and Willy and Billy and little Millie and banged their forks on the water glasses. "We want cornflakes! We want cornflakes!" they chanted.

"All we have is shredded wheat," said Ma.

"We *HATE* shredded wheat," squawked the chickens.

"What's going on here anyway?" Pa asked. "First Bossy and now you chickens. The next thing I know, the sheep will want to move in too."

"You guessed it!" said Baa-baa the black sheep.

And without even a "by your leave" as Pa said later to Ma, Baa-baa and her three cousins climbed the stairs and settled down in the hired man's room.

That was Jake Stewart. He was mighty surprised when he came in from the fields to spruce up for supper.

For a few days nothing much happened, but what with Bossy mooing and the sheep baaing and the chickens clucking and flapping around, we got awful tired.

One afternoon while he was picking up the mail, Pa felt a drowsiness coming on and when he woke up it was the next day.

Now Ma, she fell asleep everywhere. We didn't mind it at home, but on Sundays her snores shook the choir loft and rattled Reverend Dodge during silent prayer.

The only one in the place who slept good was Jake Stewart. He counted sheep every night to fall asleep. Same number every night. Four sheep.

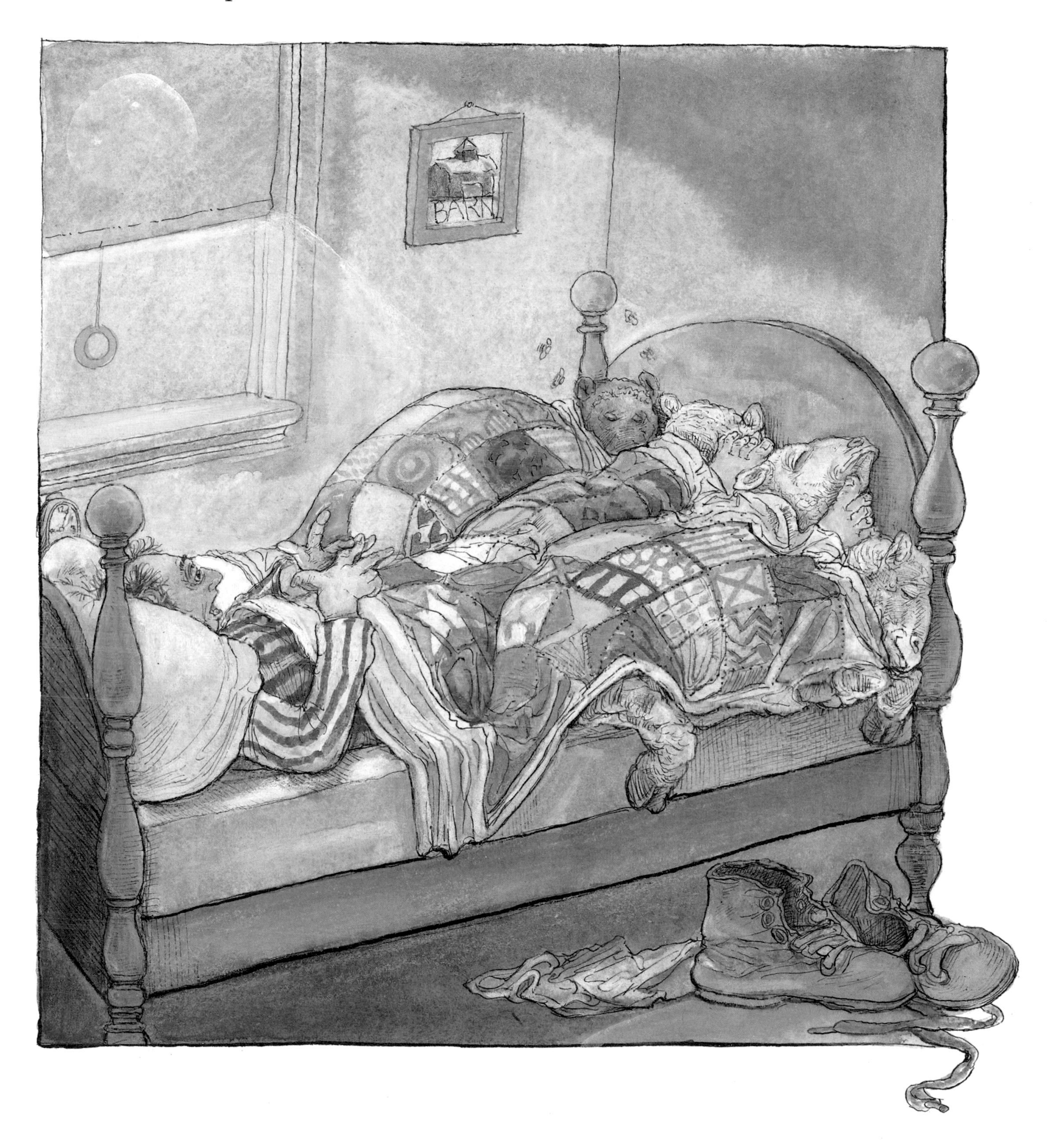

Still, we probably could have kept going that way for a long time if it hadn't been for the drought. In July no rain fell for four weeks straight and the barnyard pond dried up.

One day Ma was giving little Millie a bath when she heard a commotion at the door.

"Your time is up! It's my turn," said one pig.

"No, *me!*" said another.

"I'm next!" said the third.

Then they all took over the bathroom at once. Ma snatched up little Millie and fled.

"Calvin!" she screamed. "Calvin, come quick! The pigs are in the bathroom."

Pa was thinking about the weather. It looked a lot like rain.

"Is he deaf or something?" said Buster to Spike.

"Must be," said Spike to Buster. "She said the pigs are in the bathroom. Let's head for the house!"

Later that evening the horses were settled in front of the TV. Bossy had taken over my room and the chickens were in little Millie's, so the two of us were sleeping with the twins.

Near daybreak a dozen ducks woke us up. "Which way's the bathroom?" they demanded.

"Upstairs," said Willy.

"But the pigs are in there," said Billy.

"We'll see about THAT," quacked the ducks, and they waddled off together.

Next thing we knew, the pigs and the ducks set up an awful racket. "Ma! Pa! Wake up!" I screamed. "It's a FLOOD!"

Ma and Pa stumbled out of bed. "Someone left the water on," said Ma.

That's when the ceiling broke.

We retreated to the side yard.

"You know, Ma, I been thinking..." I said. "Seems a shame to waste our big old empty barn."

"Course it is," said Ma. "But yesterday Baa-baa told me they're pleased with Jake's room and got no intention to move."

"That's right," said Pa. "Bossy the cow said the same."

"Not them. Us," I said.

"Us?" said Willy. "You mean live in the barn?"

"Why not?" I answered. "If they like the house so much, let them have it."

Everybody started talking at once.

"You mean we wouldn't have to cook for the chickens every night?"

"Or give up our rooms?"

"Or take baths while the pigs are sleeping?"

"Or watch TV with the horses?"

"Come on!" cried Ma and Pa. "What are we waiting for? Let's start packing!"

"Just a minute there," a pig called as we were leaving. "Who's going to wash our towels?"

"Ask Buster and Spike," said Ma. "They might do it. Then again, they might not."

We drew straws to see who'd sleep where in our new home. Little Millie got the chicken coop, Billy and Willy got the hayloft, and I got Bossy's stall.

But Ma and Pa, they drew short straws and had to take the pigpen.

"I don't mind a bit," said Pa.

"Me neither," said Ma.

With no animals to take care of, we could pretty much do what we wanted. When it was sunny, we tanned on the chicken coop roof, and we swam in the barnyard pond, which was full again. On rainy days we played in the hayloft.

Our neighbors were pleased to visit us in the barn. Only Jake Stewart stayed away. People say Jake never got over the shock of finding Ma and Pa in the pigpen.

All in all it was a good summer, but 'round about November, Ma got tired of knitting sweaters and Pa got tired of whittling. Willy and Billy began to bicker something fierce, and little Millie joined in.

"There's nothing to do around here," whined the twins.
"I'm bored," whined little Millie.

Suddenly we heard a knock at the door. "We're lonely," said Bossy. "The house isn't the same without any people."

"The barn's not the same without any animals either," said Pa. "There's no cow to milk or sheep to shear or pigs to slop or horses to harness—"

"Or chickens to feed or ducks to take to water," added Ma. "We've been lonely too."

Just then I had my second idea. "How about if we move back into the house and you animals move back into the barn and start acting more like animals?"

"Suits us fine!" exclaimed the animals.

"Well then, it's agreed upon," declared Pa.

"Praise heaven," cried Ma. "Tomorrow's Thanksgiving, and I sure am mighty thankful."

"Us too! Us too!" squawked the chickens. "But before we move back, let's celebrate the holiday together up at the house."

On Thanksgiving day we were disappointed to find that the animals hadn't kept the house as neat as we might have wanted.

But we cheered up when they welcomed us in clothes from the attic and called us in to dinner.

"Hope you like it well done," said the pigs.